Bertron

Berton

GRANDMA WITHOUT ME

Story and Pictures by Judith Vigna

Albert Whitman & Company, Niles, Illinois

Text and illustrations © 1984 by Judith Vigna
Published in 1984 by Albert Whitman & Company, Niles, Illinois
Published simultaneously in Canada
by General Publishing, Limited, Toronto
All rights reserved. Printed in the United States of America.
10   9   8   7   6   5   4   3   2

The text of this book is set in sixteen-point Cheltenham Light.

Library of Congress Cataloging in Publication Data

Vigna, Judith.
   Grandma without me.

   Summary: A young boy finds a way to keep in touch
with his beloved grandmother despite his parents'
divorce.
   [1. Grandmothers—Fiction.   2. Divorce—Fiction]
I. Title.
PZ7.V67Gp 1984   [E]   83-26031
ISBN 0-8075-3030-1

I don't want Thanksgiving this year.

It won't be any fun without Grandma.
Mommy and Daddy got a divorce,
and Daddy married someone else.

Mommy says Daddy and his new wife
are going to Grandma's for Thanksgiving
this time. Grandma is Daddy's mother.
She lives far away, in another city.

I don't see why we can't go, too,
like always.
But Mommy says things are different now,
so we have to stay home.
She says I can visit Daddy's new house
whenever I want.
That's great, but I want to visit
Grandma's house again. I like my room there,
and the way Grandma fixes pancakes for me.

I don't think Mommy wants to see
Daddy and Grandma any more.
She acts like they died.

We've *never* had Thanksgiving without Grandma.
She always cooked a huge turkey,
and Mommy and Daddy and I put on funny hats.

Sometimes I ate so much I got sick.
It was the best day of my life.

When Mommy and Daddy weren't getting along,
I went to visit Grandma.
She took me lots of places.
She said the divorce wasn't my fault.
I thought I'd done something terrible.

After Daddy moved out, Grandma sent me
a scrapbook and a letter. The letter said,
My darling boy,
Your mommy doesn't want to visit
me right now. She is sad and hurt
about the divorce, just like you.
Things will get better. It will just
take time. One day we'll see each
other again. Until then, we'll keep
in touch through our scrapbook.
I will always love you.
Grandma

Grandma and I work on our scrapbook a lot.
I saved a weird purple leaf I found
and put it in the scrapbook.

Grandma sent me a feather from
her canary's cage. (Charlie molts sometimes.)

I took a picture of the new bike
Daddy got me for my birthday.

Grandma sent me a funny cartoon
she saw in the newspaper.

When I went to the Magic Show,
the magician gave me
a handkerchief for helping him.
I cut out a little piece of it
and put that in our scrapbook, too.

I can't wait to show the scrapbook to Grandma!

Y beautiful
w bike

Grandma likes
this picture

I like this
disappearing
hankerchief
better

This morning I got a mailgram,
especially for me.
It said,
  Thanksgiving won't be the same
  without my darling little boy.
  Miss you. Love and kisses from Grandma.

The man asked if the mailgram
had good news. I said yes.
It was neat of Grandma to send me
a real mailgram for our scrapbook.

She must
really miss me.

Poor Grandma!

I think I'll send her something special,
so she won't feel so bad.

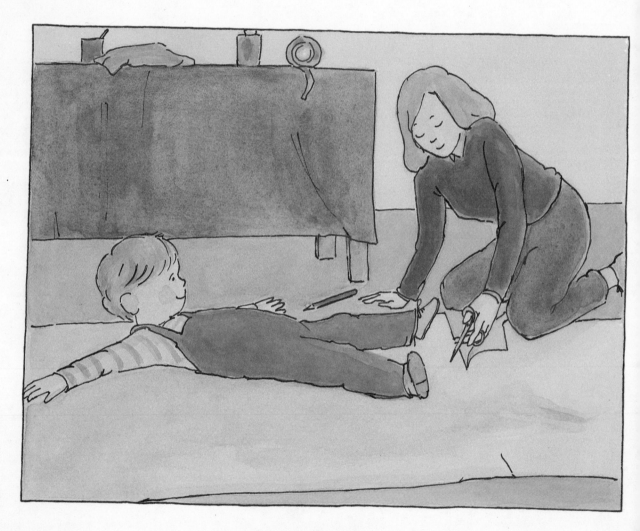

If I lie down,

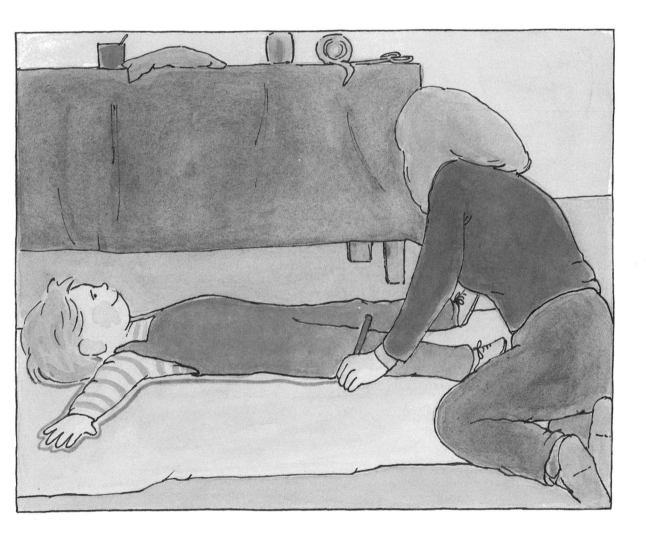

and Mommy draws around me,

Grandma can pretend I'm at her house
for Thanksgiving after all!

And *next* Thanksgiving,
Mommy's promised I'll be there for real.